The Adventures of Fancy Fae

BOOBIES GO BYE-BYE

A Weaning Story

NIKKI OSEI-BARRETT
& CYANA RILEY
Illustrated by DG

Boobies Go Bye-Bye: A Weaning Story
Copyright © 2021 by Nikki Osei-Barrett and Cyana Riley

For permissions requests, contact the publisher at www.matriarchpress.com

Library of Congress Cataloging-in-Publication data is available
ISBN: (Paperback) 979-8-218-16789-9

10 9 8 7 6 5 4 3 2
Second Printing Edition 2023

Printed in the United States of America

Original Editing, Illustrations, Book Cover Design, Layout & Formatting by DG Self-Publishing

Matriarch Press
Houston, TX
www.matriarchpress.com

MATRIARCH PRESS

Nikki's Dedication

This book is dedicated to Fancy Faye. Our twenty-two-month extended breastfeeding journey inspired this story. I'll forever cherish our nursing experience, and I'm so happy that our breastfeeding story will be told for years to come.

The book is also dedicated to my husband, Sean, my wonderful sitter, Latrice, and lastly, to Prissy Sweet Cakes - thanks for giving me the idea for the book by sliding into my DMs and saying, "Newsflash sis, *Boobies Go Bye-Bye* is definitely a book title."

Cyana's Dedication

I dedicate this book to my daughter, Teagan Riley. You were my inspiration for this book and the reason it means so much to me. Thank you for taking me on the journey of extended breastfeeding. I will forever cherish the bond we created during this special time. I love you sweet girl.

A NOTE TO WEANING MAMAS

Weaning can be a very scary change. This is the book our babies needed when it was time to transition them. We hope *Boobies Go Bye-Bye* makes the process of weaning easier and smoother for both mama and baby.

To all the mamas out there who are weaning, you got this!

When babies are born,
they need milk to grow.
Milk helps make them strong
from their head to their toe.

When Fancy Faye was a baby,
she loved milk from Mama's breast.
She snuggled close, she cuddled near,
in Mama's arms she felt the best.

Milk from Mama's boobies made Fancy Faye happy,
and helped her calm down when she was sad.
Mama's milk was the best comfort
that Fancy Faye had.

Milk from Mama's boobies made Fancy Faye

GROW

and

GROW

and **GROW**

She was almost
too big for
Mama's lap,
and it was
starting to show.

Mama looked down at Fancy Faye,
and she felt sad, it's true.
Her baby had grown so very much.
Mama knew what she had to do.

Mama hugged Fancy Faye close to her
as she drank Mama's milk one last time.
With a tear,
Mama looked at Fancy Faye and said,
"It's time for Mama's boobies to go bye-bye."

The next day, something strange
caught Fancy Faye by surprise:

Mama's boobies had Band-Aids on them.
She could not believe her eyes!

Mama looked at Fancy Faye and said,
"I'm sorry, my girl. I don't want to make you cry,

but Mama's boobies
are broken.
It's time for boobies
to go bye-bye."

Fancy Faye was so very sad,
and she cried big tears.
But Mama was right there for her
to help ease her fears.

Mama kept Fancy Faye close to her,
and held her so very tight.
Mama whispered to Fancy Faye softly,
and told her it would be all right.

"New things can be scary;
they scare Mama too.
But Fancy Faye's a big girl now
with big girl things to do."

Fancy Faye was sad,
but she understood.
She handled it like a big girl,
just like Mama knew she would.

"It's time for boobies to go bye-bye.
I know it's hard to let them go,
but they've already done their job
by making Fancy Faye grow.
And now it's time for
Mama's boobies to go bye-bye.

Mama's milk is not here to stay.
The day has come for Mama's milk to go away.
Mama's boobies go bye-bye."

Fancy Faye's a big girl now,
she is all grown up.
Fancy Faye has big-girl milk
inside her big-girl cup.

Fancy Faye eats yummy foods,
she's growing every day.
She loves to have fun with big brother Nick.
They run and jump and play.

Mama's boobies have gone away,
and it really is okay!
Mama's proud of Fancy Faye
and she loves her in every way.

And Mama's love will never go bye-bye.

AUTHOR BIOS

Nikki Osei-Barrett is a wife, mom, and entrepreneur hailing from the DMV. She's married to her high school sweetheart, is a teen mom success story, and a mother to three beautiful children. Nikki is an HBCU grad representing Bowie State University. She's a strategic communicator and owner of Osei PR, a boutique fashion, beauty, and lifestyle PR agency. She is also the co-founder of District Motherhued®, a nonprofit which caters to millennial moms of color, and The Momference®, the nation's first full-scale conference for Black moms. Nikki is proud to add "children's author" to her list of titles.

Cyana Riley was born and raised in Washington, DC. She graduated from George Washington University and spent the first six years of her career as a teacher. It was during that time that she fell in love with writing and sharing children's stories. Cyana is also the author of *Not So Different*, an Amazon bestseller. Cyana is a stay-at-home mom, currently residing in Maryland with her husband and two beautiful children.

SHARE YOUR FEEDBACK!

Did you enjoy this book? Please post a review on Amazon to let others know about your experience. Your review will help get this book into the hands of more children. We would love to hear your feedback!

Made in the USA
Las Vegas, NV
27 October 2023

79812148R00021